P9-CCX-234

MOLEHOLE MYSTERIES

THE GYPSIES' SECRET

WRITTEN BY

Barbara Davoll

Pictures by Dennis Hockerman

© 1992 by
BARBARA DAVOLL

All rights reserved. No part of this book may be reproduced
in any form without permission in writing from the publisher,
except in the case of brief quotations embodied in critical articles
or reviews.

Moody Press, a ministry of the Moody Bible Institute,
is designed for education, evangelization, and edifi-
cation. If we may assist you in knowing more about
Christ and the Christian life, please write us without
obligation: Moody Press, c/o MLM, Chicago, IL 60610.
Printed in MEXICO.

ISBN: 0-8024-2702-2

Children love the stories of Barbara Davoll, known for her award-winning, best-selling Christopher Churchmouse Classics and now for the Molehole Mystery series. Barbara writes these zany new adventures in Schroon Lake, New York where she and her husband, Roy, minister at home and abroad with Word of Life International in their Missions Department. Barb manages to stay busy as a wife, mother, grandmother, author, drama teacher, church musician, and homemaker for her husband and Josh, the family Schnauzer.

Illustrator Dennis Hockerman has concentrated on art for children's trade books and textbooks, magazines, greeting cards, and games. He lives with his wife and three children in Mequon, Wisconsin, a suburb of Milwaukee. Mr. Hockerman probably spent more time "underground" than above while developing the characters and creating the etchings for the Molehole Mysteries. Periodically, he would poke his head into his "upstairs connection" to join his family and share with them the adventures of his friends in Molesbury R.F.D.

Contents

MURDOCH MOLE, ESQUIRE

Dusty Mole sat hunched over the toadstool that served as his desk, writing in his journal. Things had been very busy at the Molehole Mystery Club lately, and he had not had time to enter all the mysteries solved in his detective's diary.

The junior agent scratched his head and thought back over the past few days. *I must remember to write in my journal every day. It's too hard trying to remember all the details after the mysteries are solved.*

The little mole was so busy he didn't hear the door of the clubhouse open. Standing in front of him was a large, well-dressed gentleman mole wearing a pin-striped business suit and carrying a leather briefcase. The large mole was peering at him through an eyeglass.

"My dear sir," drawled the impressive looking animal. "I am looking for a private detective named Dusty Mole. Can you direct me to him, if you please?"

"I am Dusty Mole," answered the detective, putting aside his notebook and rising to greet the caller.

The large mole took a step backward and said, "Come now, young fellow, I'm sure this cannot be true. I was *told* Dusty Mole is a man of experience, not a mere *boy* such as yourself."

Dusty smiled, determined not to be upset by this rude animal. "Well, I'm not an adult mole, but I have had some experience. I'm a junior agent and—"

"Sir! You are talking with Murdoch Mole, Esquire! I demand to be put in contact immediately with the one in charge of this—this sorry business," sputtered the proud animal. He peered through his eyeglass at the clubhouse as if it had a bad smell.

Suddenly Dusty was aware of the holes in the wall, the dusty floor, and the shabby appearance of the room in which they stood.

"I am the one in charge, Mr. Murdoch," answered the little mole. "May I be of some help to you?"

"Well, this is not at all what I expected. But that isn't important if you can give me some information."

"I'll be happy to assist in any way I can," answered Dusty politely. "Won't you have a seat?" He pulled up a chair and dusted it off.

"Thank you. I will sit down for a moment," answered the haughty mole, sitting down carefully on the edge of the chair. Opening the briefcase he took out a picture of a young boy mole and laid it on the table in front of Dusty.

"This is my son, Millard,"
he stated. "He has been
kidnapped."

"Are you certain of that?"
questioned Dusty.

"Sir! You are speaking with Murdoch Mole. I am
always certain when I speak."

"Forgive me for questioning you," apologized Dusty.
"You see, if I am to help, there are things I must know.
May I ask you some questions?"

"I suppose you must," drawled Murdoch. "Proceed."

"Are you certain your son, Millard, was kidnapped?"
asked the mole detective again.

"Well, he is missing from our home, so I assume so,"
answered the father. "And at a very bad time too."

"What do you mean by that?" inquired Dusty, who
was making notes in his clues journal as they spoke.

"Well, I mean it is a terribly inconvenient time for
him to disappear. I am trying to close a very large
business deal amounting to a small fortune. My wife
was to entertain her garden club for tea today. But all
has been postponed because that rascal of a boy has
been kidnapped."

"Did you receive a ransom note from his kidnappers?" asked Dusty.

"Well, no," drawled Murdoch impatiently. "But I am sure that it is so. You see, his clothing, toys—everything he owns—were left behind."

"When was that?" questioned Dusty.

The wealthy mole shifted his weight on the chair and looked away. "We're not really sure," he admitted.

"You aren't *sure*?" exclaimed the detective. "How old is your son?"

"He is eight years old," mumbled Murdoch meekly.

"How can a father not know when his son disappeared?"

"I'm gone from home a lot," explained the large mole.

"Well, I'm sure Millard's mother must know when he was last seen. I will need to question her as well," stated the junior agent, writing in his notebook.

"She doesn't know either," explained the embarrassed father. "She has been gone a lot too. Only the servants were home, and they can't remember when they last saw him."

Dusty leaned back in his chair and looked at the well-to-do mole. *What kind of a family is this?* he wondered. *How can I help them if they don't have any clues to give me?*

MURDOCH MOLE'S MANSION

Dusty could see he was getting nowhere questioning Murdoch Mole. The large mole had no ideas or clues about his son.

"Mr. Murdoch, I suggest that I also question your wife. Perhaps together you can give me some idea what has happened to your son. May I call at your home this evening?"

The proud businessman stood to his feet and snapped his briefcase shut. "You have Millard's picture," he said. "That should help you find him quickly. Surely the kidnappers can't have gone far. After all, this part of our underground is not very large."

"Mr. Murdoch, I'm sorry but I won't be able to take your case," said the mole detective firmly. "I cannot find Millard without your cooperation. You will have to go to the police."

The embarrassed mole began to sputter. "The po-police! Never! Why that could ruin me if they find out about this scandal! I came to you to find my son, and I insist that you do so immediately!"

Dusty shook his head sadly. "No, Mr. Murdoch. I cannot work under such pressure. I won't accept your case unless I can question all of those involved with your son."

"Oh, all right!" exploded the proud animal. "We will be home at seven this evening. You may come at that time. We will give you one hour for questions." And with that he stormed from the room, nearly colliding with Snarkey Mole, a member of the Molehole Mystery Club gang.

"Well, pahdon *me*," said Snarkey, mocking the funny way Mr. Murdoch spoke. He stepped quickly out of the large mole's path. "Who was that?"

"Murdoch Mole, Esquire," Dusty informed him. "He insists his son has been kidnapped, but he can't tell me when he was last seen or where."

"Sounds like a case of parent neglect to me," said Snarkey.

"Hmm. Perhaps. I'm going to their home to question him and his wife tonight. I *hope* I'll find out more."

"Better you than me," responded Snarkey. "I have trouble with those who think they're better than anyone else."

"Well, I sure don't have a good first impression of him," agreed Dusty. "I think I'll take Musty with me. She can charm the sox off anybody. Perhaps she'll do better with the Murdoch Moles than I will."

Later that evening the twin moles approached the address that was on the back of Millard's picture. Musty drew in her breath as she saw the huge pillars, beautiful fountains, and flowers that were in front of the Murdoch Mole home.

"They must have a lot of money, Dusty. Where did they get all these flowers?" asked the little girl mole with wonder. "Flowers don't grow in the underground."

"I guess they got them from 'upstairs'," said her brother. "Can you imagine having that kind of money? Must cost them a fortune to bring them down here and keep them fresh."

"What does Murdoch Mole do?" asked Musty, bending low over a beautiful rose to smell it.

"I learned this afternoon that he is in the oil business. They say he has the whole underground oil supply in his control."

"No wonder this is such a beautiful home," Musty exclaimed. "Millard could have been kidnapped," she reasoned. "Kidnappers are always after the rich to get their money."

Dusty pulled on the brass doorbell. They could hear the chime ringing inside the house. The door was opened by a stately butler, who looked with suspicion down his long mole nose.

"Whom shall I say is calling?" he inquired stiffly.

"Dusty and Musty Mole, junior agents," answered the detective.

"Dusty! Take a look at this home!" whispered Musty, as the butler went to announce them. "I've never seen anything like this in my life!"

"The Murdoch Moles are in the library," said the butler as he returned, showing them to a large open doorway.

The two junior agents walked through the doorway into a beautiful room lined with books from floor to ceiling. A warm fire was burning in the fireplace to take the chill off the underground home.

Seated on an elegant chair by the fireplace was a small mole lady dressed in beautiful clothing. Around her dainty neck was the most dazzling necklace Musty had ever seen. The jewels were nearly blinding as they caught the light from the fire.

Standing in front of the fireplace was Murdoch Mole, now dressed in casual clothes. His face plainly showed the worry he felt over Millard. It was evident that Mrs. Murdoch had been crying. She quickly dabbed her eyes with a delicate lace hanky as she saw them come in.

Musty's heart was pounding as they approached the wealthy moles. Their riches made her feel uneasy. A side glance at her twin brother told her he was uneasy too. He was pushing his glasses up on his nose the way he always did when he was nervous.

There's no need to be nervous, Musty told herself. *They're just moles like we are.* She wished she could make herself believe that.

THE MISSING MOLE

"Come in, sir," drawled Murdoch. "I'm afraid you find us in a very upset condition. My dear wife is nearly beside herself with worry over Millard." He walked over to his wife and patted her shoulder awkwardly.

"Mr. Murdoch, this is my sister, Musty," said Dusty. "She is my partner, and I thought it would be helpful for her to talk with your wife. Sometimes ladies can talk to each other easier than to us men."

"Quite right," agreed Murdoch, who seemed to be in a much more humble state of mind than when he first met Dusty. He took Musty's paw and brought her closer to his wife. "Look dear, this is, uh—Musty Mole —who has come to talk to you about Millard."

Mrs. Murdoch looked up with tear-filled eyes. "Thank you for coming," she said quietly. "I will be so grateful if you can help us find my little son."

"We will certainly try," said Musty encouragingly.

Mr. Murdoch indicated that Musty should seat herself beside his wife. "Please make yourself comfortable. Dusty and I can talk over here." He led the way to a comfortable couch nearby.

Musty took out her notebook and began to talk quietly with Mrs. Murdoch. "Can you tell me when you last saw Millard?" she questioned. The little mole detective waited patiently for Mrs. Murdoch to answer.

"I—I can't remember," said the beautiful mole lady brokenly. "You see, I always leave him in the care of our servants. Some—sometimes I don't see him for days." At this she began to cry harder.

Musty was shocked! Whoever heard of a mother who didn't see her child for days? With a sick feeling inside, she wrote the fact down in her notebook.

"Is it possible to question the servants?" Musty asked Mrs. Murdoch.

"Certainly. But I'm afraid they don't know much. I've already asked them when they last saw Millard. The nurse thinks she saw him playing outside two days ago.

"The cook said the last time she saw him was when he begged for some bread to feed his pet mouse. She refused to give him any as it was near supper. She was afraid Millard might eat the bread himself and spoil his supper.

"The butler says he knows Millard didn't go out with anyone. Jeeves always keeps the doors locked. There are thieves around who might steal our valuables," she explained.

"The gardener can't remember exactly when he saw him last. He did say there was one day last week when Millard's ball went in the rose garden. He remembers because he was very upset that Millard tramped on some of his prize roses. He said he told him he was a naughty boy and that the rose garden was off limits to him."

"Does Millard have any friends who come to play with him?" questioned Musty. Her heart was breaking for this poor little rich mole, who seemed to be in everybody's way.

"No," answered Mrs. Murdoch sadly. "You see, we've always been very careful because we were afraid he would be kidnapped. His father never felt any of the children in town were—were good enough to play with Millard." She looked over at her husband and Dusty, who were deep in serious talk.

"Murdoch doesn't like a lot of noise," she said in a whisper. "He always wanted Millard to be quiet. We didn't allow him to play with other mole children."

Musty stared at the little mole lady who was crying into her hanky again. *What a sad, lonely life Millard has had*, she thought.

"What about school, Mrs. Murdoch? Millard surely went to school, didn't he?"

"Oh yes. He went to the Molehole Elementary School every morning. During the summer, we allowed him to go to the school's youth center for their sports program. We let him walk, as it isn't very far. He had a little key around his neck, and that way he didn't have to trouble anyone when he came home. He could let himself in the door. Our cook was supposed to have milk and cookies waiting for him in his room."

"So no one even saw him when he came home?" questioned Musty.

Mrs. Murdoch shook her head and broke into fresh crying at this. "Oh, I've thought a thousand times how wrong we've been. We bought everything for him, but I was so busy with all my club work. I was gone every day, and every night there was something we had to do.

"Murdoch wanted things quiet and dignified," she said, crying. "Well, it's very quiet now," she sobbed. Our Millard is gone."

THE MISSING CLUE

After a few more questions Dusty and Musty left the Murdoch Mole home. They really knew little more than they had before they came. Neither parent seemed to know much about their son, and the servants were unwilling to answer questions.

"I think I'd fire that cook and nurse," stormed Musty as they walked home. "When I asked them about Millard they acted strangely—as if it were too much trouble to even answer a few questions about the missing little mole."

"The gardener wasn't any help either," agreed Dusty. "All he seemed to care about was Millard chasing his ball into his rose garden. He kept informing me how much money it costs everyday to have those flowers brought down from the upstairs."

"That snooty butler is something else too," fumed Musty. "He has the longest nose of any mole I know!"

"You're right!" added Dusty. "He sure knows how to make you feel like two cents, doesn't he? 'Pahdon me, sir, but you're getting nasty dirt on our white carpeting'."

Musty laughed at Dusty's mockery of the stiff butler. "You'd almost think he wasn't a mole, he puts on such airs!"

"Poor Millard." Dusty sighed. "Can you imagine how lonely he must have been living there? He's probably *glad* he was kidnapped—if he was."

"Do *you* think he was kidnapped?" asked Musty.

"I don't know," admitted Dusty. "How are we ever going to find any clues? No one knows a thing about him."

"Well, we can check with the coach at the school. He's been enrolled in their summer games program. He'll know when Millard was last there," reasoned Musty.

"We'll do that first thing in the morning," said her brother. "Right now I just want to get home and see Mother Miranda and Father. I'm so glad we aren't rich," he added with a shake of his head. "We may not have a lot of money, but we sure have fun back in our little molehole."

"You said it," agreed Musty. "Let's go! We still have time to play some games before bedtime."

The next morning the twins visited the Molehole Youth Center. Millard's coach was upset that he was missing. He had not been to practice for three days, and the coach had just thought he was sick.

"Millard is a well-behaved, quiet mole and an excellent athlete," he told them. "There are times that he seems very lonely though. He doesn't have many friends and is usually alone."

"Do his parents come to the games?" asked Musty.

"No, I've never met them," responded the coach. "They always send the butler to pick him up after we have a game. No one is ever here to cheer for him. I've always felt that was too bad. The butler even signs his permission slips for the away games."

The junior agents left the youth center feeling very discouraged.

"Now what?" questioned Musty. "Where do we go from here?"

"I guess we'll just have to take his picture and ask animals on the street if they've seen him," suggested Dusty.

However, a full day of doing that got them nowhere. No one they questioned had seen the little mole.

"You know, Musty, I think we should go to the police. This is getting very serious," said Dusty with concern.

"Yes, it is," agreed his partner. "But won't that upset Murdoch? He didn't want the police to get in on it."

"Frankly, I don't care," responded Dusty. "I'm concerned that we find his son. It almost seems that he's more concerned about his reputation than finding Millard. I say we go to the police."

Just then Otis, a member of the Molehole Mystery Club, rounded the corner in a great hurry, nearly knocking them over.

"Dusty! Am I glad to see you! I've been looking everywhere for you," he panted. Otis was chubby, and such activity was a bit unusual for him.

"Hi, Otis! What's up?" asked Dusty.

"I've been looking for clues ever since you told us about the missing mole kid," said Otis with excitement. "Guess what I found out?" he asked mysteriously.

"Dusty and I are all ears, Otis," responded Musty. "We haven't been able to discover anything at all."

"You know that snooty butler of the Murdoch Moles?"

The twins looked at each other and nodded their heads.

"I found out he has a police record. He was in jail once for stealing some silver where he used to work," said Otis.

A startled look passed between Dusty and his sister. *Could that be the missing clue? Perhaps the butler is the kidnapper!*

THE GYPSIES' CART

Musty was the first to react to Otis's information that Murdoch Mole's butler had a police record.

"I just *knew* he was guilty the way he acted!" she said. "I bet he's the one who kidnapped Millard, and he'll send a ransom note later to get money out of them."

"Whoa! Not so fast, sis. Just because the butler made a mistake once doesn't mean he's guilty now," responded her always cautious brother.

"I don't know, Dusty. Sounds reasonable to me," said Otis. "At least it's something to check out."

"That it is, Otis. Good work! I'll put you on that detail. See what you can find out about the butler. Find out when he was in jail, where he lived and worked before here. Don't overlook anything."

"Right!" said Otis. "I'll report to the Club tomorrow afternoon with what I find." With that he scooted off to search for any clue to the missing Millard.

"Why don't we see what we can dig up about the butler too, Dusty?" said his twin. "This is the best thing we have to go on so far."

"Uh—sure, Musty. You do that. I have some other things to work on this afternoon. See you later!"

Musty stood staring after her brother, feeling a bit as though she had been dismissed. *Now what can he be doing?* she wondered. If she knew her brother, he had some clue up his sleeve. *I guess I'll have to find some clues on my own.* She determined that she would turn up something helpful that day and set off in the direction of the Murdoch Mole mansion.

As Musty scooted along she thought over everything that had been said the night before at Murdoch's home. It certainly seemed possible that the butler knew more about Millard than they had thought. That would explain his being unwilling to answer their questions.

Musty was approaching Millard's home when she heard voices behind the shrubs that surrounded the beautiful mansion.

The girl mole stopped and tried to listen. She recognized the voices of the butler and gardener.

"Do you suppose those two detective moles will find the little brat?" asked the gardener. "I'm just as glad not to have him around. He makes a lot of extra work for me, messing up the flower gardens."

"Naw! I figure he's gone for good. They can look all they want, but I doubt if we'll be troubled with him again," answered the butler.

Musty stood with a shocked look on her face. *The butler and gardener are in it together,* she thought excitedly. *I've got to find Dusty and tell him what I heard!*

Meanwhile Dusty was searching for his own clues. He had decided to find out all he could about the father, Murdoch Mole. The boy mole was on his way to the underground oil supply where Millard's father worked. Perhaps a few questions there might shed some light about the missing little mole.

As Dusty walked along he spotted a brightly colored cart ahead on the side of the road. The cart, which was drawn by a team of snails, was sitting lop-sided as though it had broken down. When Dusty got closer he could see that a wheel from the cart was broken. A couple of moles, dressed in strange looking clothing, were trying to fix the wheel.

"Good afternoon," said Dusty politely. "Having a bit of trouble, I see. May I help in any way?"

"We trying to fix our wheel," said one mole, who wore loose-fitting orange pants, a beautiful pink shirt, and a colorful sash about his waist. His speech was difficult to understand. *Must be from another part of the underground*, thought Dusty.

"Let me have a look," said Dusty, stooping to see if he could help fix the wheel.

"Hmm, looks as though you may need another one," he said. "This wheel can't be fixed, I'm afraid. Are you from around here?"

"No, we just travel through Molesbury. We camp outside town," said the other mole, who had a long mustache and a scarf tied around his head. "We are gypsies," explained the second mole.

Gypsies! thought Dusty. He had heard stories about gypsies being dishonest. He had heard they often would kidnap and then try to get large amounts of ransom money from the families of those kidnapped. *Now maybe I'm getting somewhere. Maybe these gypsies are behind Millard's disappearance.*

MILLARD MOLE'S HAT

Dusty stared with fascination at the moles standing in front of him. Although he had often heard of gypsies he had never seen any. He knew they traveled about from place to place.

"It very bad our wagon is broke," one said. "We live in our wagons," he explained.

"I'm sorry," said Dusty. "I'd be glad to let you stay with my family and me in Molesbury tonight. Perhaps we can find another wheel for you." As he said this he wondered if it would be wise to have them in his home.

"You are so kind," said the first gypsy, "but I must get back to camp to my wife and little ones. They be wondering where we are. We go on there and see what we do. Thank you for offer though," he said, and bowing politely they started to leave.

"Oh, wait a minute," called Dusty, taking Millard's picture from his pocket. "I'm looking for a young mole who is missing from his home. Have you seen him?" he asked, showing them Millard's picture.

Both gypsies looked at the picture and quickly said they had not. Dusty noticed that they now seemed nervous and anxious to get away.

"By the way, my name is Dusty Mole, junior agent of the Molehole Mystery Club. If you see Millard, please let me know," said Dusty, putting the picture back in his pocket.

"Yah! We be sure to do that," they said. In a comical way they tripped over each other, trying to hurry away.

Dusty scratched his head and looked after them as they scurried down the road. He was convinced they knew something about Millard, as they had acted so strangely when he showed them his picture.

Their brightly colored wagon leaned on its broken wheel. Suddenly Dusty noticed that the tool they had been using to repair the broken wheel was lying in the road.

I'd better put this inside their wagon, he thought. *Somebody might steal it if I leave it here in the road.*

Dusty picked up the tool, walked around to the other side of the wagon, and opened the door of the little trailer. As he laid the tool inside on the floor he looked around the neat little cart that served as their home.

A small table and chairs, a tiny bed, and a few items of clothing were all arranged in neat order. Lying on the table was something that caught the eye of the experienced detective mole. Dusty stared at the item and then drew the picture of Millard Mole from his pocket.

Lying on the table was a hat exactly like the one Millard was wearing in the picture. *That has to be Millard's hat,* thought Dusty with excitement. *There can't be another one like that in all of Molesbury. Perhaps I should pay a call to that gypsy camp outside of town.* Somehow he knew the gypsies were involved with Millard's disappearance.

THE GYPSY KING

Dusty closed the door to the gypsy wagon and started quickly down the road in the direction the gypsies had gone. They were already out of sight, but he knew they couldn't be far ahead.

The junior agent followed the gypsy moles, being careful that they not know he was following. Soon a wide clearing appeared. In the clearing was a large number of gypsy carts. The gypsies turned into their camp, and Dusty darted behind some tree roots, staying out of sight.

Dusty could hear laughter, loud singing, and strange music such as he'd never heard before. From behind the clump of roots he could see and hear everything going on in the gypsy camp.

In the midst of the carts a group of gypsies was singing and swaying to violin music. The gypsy mole who was playing the violin played with such beauty that the sound nearly made Dusty cry.

Gypsy mothers held their babies and rocked them to the beautiful music. Gypsy men held their children and sang in voices tender with love and emotion. When the music ended, all clapped, cheering and congratulating the one who played the violin. They seemed so happy and cheerful that Dusty longed to join them.

Suddenly strong paws clasped him, and a deep voice said, "Come with us!"

Dusty's heart began to pound. He had been captured by two large gypsy moles. Long knives hung from their waists. They shoved him roughly into the center of the ring of wagons. The gypsies, who only minutes before had been so loving and happy, now turned silent cold stares on him.

Dusty's fur was standing straight up. He could feel danger around him. As he was thrown to the ground he was astounded to see Millard Mole staring down at him. Millard was dressed as a gypsy and stood with his paws across his chest looking at Dusty with eyes of suspicion.

"Millard Mole!" exclaimed the detective.

A look of surprise crossed the face of the mole, but he did not change his position.

"What are you doing here?" demanded Dusty.

"*I live here,*" said Millard firmly. "And my name is *not* Millard Mole. My name is Raoul."

"But you are—or *were*—Millard Mole, weren't you?" asked Dusty in his best junior agent voice. He had forgotten his fear and the danger he was facing in the excitement of finding Millard.

"Answer him nothing!" exploded one of the men who had captured him. "You talk only to our leader."

A flurry of excitement passed through the gypsies as a large imposing mole stepped into the ring. He was clothed in beautiful rich clothing with spangles and jewels. Gold slippers, turned up at the toes, were on his feet, and he wore several gold rings.

"I am Fernando, king of the gypsies," he said in perfect English. "Why have you come to our camp?"

"My name is Dusty Mole, and I have been looking for Millard Mole. I am a junior detective agent. I met two of your gypsies on the way here and followed them to see if Millard might be among you. I see I was not wrong," he added, looking at Millard.

"Millard, as you call him, has joined us," explained
the gypsy king. "His name is now Raoul. We do not
question his right to join us if he wishes."

"I'm certain he *joined* you because you kidnapped
him," accused Dusty. "I have heard that you kidnap
and steal!" His eyes snapped with anger.

"Gypsies do not kidnap!" exploded the king. "Nor
do we steal or do other bad things as some say. We
are not bad animals!" His fur bristled.

"It certainly looks like it," accused Dusty further. "This young mole's parents have asked me to find their son. They are very worried about him."

As Dusty said this Millard looked down as if ashamed.

"We do not keep him," insisted the leader. "He is free to go!" he exclaimed with a sweeping motion toward Millard.

"Well then," said Dusty with relief, "let's be on our way, Millard."

"I—I do not wish to leave," said Millard in a small voice.

"You don't want to go home?" exclaimed Dusty in surprise.

"No, I don't," insisted the little mole. "I ran away to join the gypsies when I saw what love and happiness they have here. I was very lonely. My new name is Raoul, and this is now my home."

"But what will I tell your parents, Millard? They love you very much, you know."

Millard shifted his feet uncomfortably in the sand and then said sadly, "They never *said* they did."

Dusty didn't know how to answer the poor little mole. *What can I say to that?* thought Dusty. *How can I convince him that he should come home?*

"Millard," said Dusty quietly, "I know it may seem your parents did not care for you because they were so busy. But they really do love you. Sometimes parents make mistakes. I know they are very sorry they haven't spent more time with you. I just saw them. Both were so worried about you they were crying."

At that the little mole's eyes filled with tears. "Even my father?" he asked.

"Even your father," answered Dusty.

"He gave me this key!" Millard spat angrily, ripping the key from his neck and throwing it to the ground. "He doesn't care where I am or when I come and go. He doesn't love me!" he cried. Angry tears washed down the face of the miserable little mole.

"That really isn't true," argued Dusty. "He thought you were being cared for by the servants. It seemed important to him to buy things for you, so he worked very hard to get money. I've talked with your parents, and both now see they have been wrong about many things.

"It is your place as a son to obey and love your parents, no matter what. You must forgive them. It was very wrong for you to run away and join these gypsies."

The two gypsies with the long knives moved forward as Dusty said this. "Shall we take care of him?" they asked the leader, with their hands on their knives.

8

THE RANSOM NOTE

As Dusty faced the men with the knives and the gypsy king, he thought perhaps he had gone too far.

The king put up his hand to stop the gypsy men from harming Dusty. "No! We do not deal with force! I must think," he said. He began to walk around the wagon circle in deep thought. At last he stopped and stood before Dusty once again.

"I have decided. We will demand a ransom," he said simply.

"But—but you said you don't kidnap!" sputtered Dusty. "You must be kidnappers to demand a ransom!"

"No, my young friend. Not a ransom as you suppose. I shall write the ransom note." With a gesture the king called for paper, and soon he had written a note, which he thrust at Dusty.

The note was very surprising to the junior agent. It said, "To the parents of Millard Mole. Your son has joined the gypsy band of which Fernando Gao is king. These gypsies are camped at the south edge of Molesbury. The ransom for you to reclaim your child is threefold: First, Murdoch Mole and his wife must present themselves to these gypsies and give valid reason why their son should rejoin them. Second, they also must give promise and proof that sufficient time and love will be given to Millard. Third, Millard must forgive his parents and gladly become their son again. Signed, Fernando Gao, King of Gypsies."

"This is very good, sir," said Dusty to the king. "You have shown great understanding and wisdom. I am sorry for the way I have accused you."

The king nodded, accepting his apology. "Many people think the same as you because they do not really know us. The little one has told us much. Money cannot buy love.

"The child has been very lonely in the Murdoch Mole home. Their servants are uncaring, and he has been left to himself. It is understandable that he doesn't wish to go home. We care deeply about him and want only his best."

Turning to Millard he said, "My little friend, it is right for you to go home. You will remember, I said you might stay until you knew our secret. That secret is love," said the king softly.

"Love is that which makes us a family. Love will give you the strength to forgive your parents. It is the strength that will help them admit they have been wrong, and it will change your home to a happy one. We will await their coming."

With that the king bowed deeply, and the two gypsies with the knives escorted Dusty to the edge of the clearing. Dusty quickly made his way down the road to the Murdoch Mole home, clutching the ransom note in his paw.

Murdoch will get his ransom note, but it won't be what he expects, he thought.

As Dusty approached Murdoch's home he heard a familiar hiss. "Musty!" he exclaimed in surprise. "What are you doing here?"

"Sh!" said Musty, coming from behind the bushes. "They'll hear you. I know who kidnapped Millard," she said with pride.

"You do?" exclaimed Dusty in surprise. "How can you? I just got the ransom note myself. How can you know already?"

"Huh?" said Musty. "Why I heard the butler and gardener talking about how they disliked Millard and—"

"No, Musty," interrupted her brother, trying not to lose patience. "They had nothing to do with it. I've just seen Millard, and I have a ransom note from the gypsies for Murdoch."

"Yes!" cried Musty, not even hearing what Dusty had said. "I figured it all out myself, and I—what did you say? You saw whom?"

"That's what I said, sis. I just saw Millard at a gypsy camp, and I have a ransom note here with me." Dusty held out the note for Musty to read.

She read it quickly and listened as he told her the details about Millard and the gypsies.

"Shucks!" she said in a disappointed voice. "I thought I had it all figured out!"

"Well, never mind," said her brother. "Come on in with me, and let's give them the note. The important thing is that we know where he is and that he's all right."

When the two little moles handed the ransom note to Murdoch he took it saying, "I knew it. I just knew he'd been kidnapped!"

Dusty looked at his sister and shook his head. *Wait till Murdoch finds out Millard wasn't kidnapped,* he thought.

THE GYPSY CAMP

"Well, let's see how much they want," said the father. "I knew we'd get a ransom note sooner or later."

As he read the note Murdoch's paw shook and he sank onto the couch. "I can't believe it," he said. "They could have demanded any amount from me."

"There are some things money can't buy, sir," said Dusty.

"Are you *sure* he wasn't kidnapped? Maybe this is a trap to get us out there and—"

"This is not a trap, Murdoch," said Dusty firmly. "Your son ran away."

"Oh, what is it?" cried the mother mole, coming in. "Is my boy dead?" she wailed.

Her husband handed her the note, and as she read it she too began to shake.

"Oh, my dear little son! Is he safe there?" she asked anxiously.

"Quite safe," assured Dusty. "In fact, he is very loved and happy." Then Dusty filled in the details about his changed name and how their son didn't want to come home.

Tears ran down the mother mole's face, and the father appeared deep in thought. Tears also stood in his eyes.

"I can't believe he'd run away. To think he was that lonely," said Murdoch in disbelief. "Let's go, Mother. We have to face it. It's true, we haven't been the best parents. We need to make things right with our son and see if we can get our family back together."

With Musty helping Mrs. Murdoch, they made their way to the gypsy camp. When she saw Millard dressed in his gypsy clothing she began to cry and run toward him. Throwing her arms around him she cried, "Oh, my little son. I'm so glad to find you."

The missing boy mole stood stiffly and allowed himself to be hugged. He looked coldly at his mother and said, "My name is Raoul. This is now my home."

Dusty looked wildly between Millard and his parents. *Oh no!* he thought. *How are we going to overcome this?*

"Uh—hello, son," said Murdoch, putting out his paw awkwardly to shake.

Millard didn't budge an inch.

"Uh—son—your mother and I want to ask you to forgive us. We supposed you were happy at home and the servants were—"

"Were what, Mr. Murdoch?" All eyes turned to see King Fernando standing quietly beside Millard. "You *supposed* the servants were doing the job you should have been doing as parents? There is no substitute, my dear sir, for love and care from your own parents."

At this Mrs. Murdoch began to cry openly. Millard shifted around, looking embarrassed at his mother's tears.

"Look at the misery you're causing your mother, Millard," began her husband. "I demand that you—"

Murdoch stopped speaking in the middle of his sentence as the king put up his hand and spoke.

"It seems you have a problem, sir. Your son has said he prefers to live here where there is love and caring. If you are to meet the demands of the ransom note, something must be done to bring the three of you together."

"I can see that," mumbled Murdoch humbly. "What is your suggestion, Dusty?" asked the wealthy man, looking at the junior agent.

"Well, I—" began Dusty.

To Dusty's relief the king interrupted. "I have a suggestion, sir, which I hope you will accept. I would suggest that you and your wife remain with us here in our camp for a few days' vacation. I think you would enjoy yourselves. You will be able to see how we function as families and care for our children. What would you say to that?"

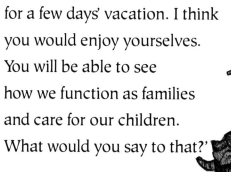

Dusty saw Millard looking at his father hopefully. *I think he wants them to stay,* thought the agent with excitement. *Maybe this will be just what they all need.*

"What do you say, dear?" Murdoch asked his wife. "Will that be all right with you?"

"Why—I don't know. Where would we sleep?" asked the mother.

"Oh, you may have my large wagon," said the king. "You will find it comfortable, I'm sure."

"Of course we would pay—"

"No!" said the king firmly. "There is no need for money here. This will be our gift of love to your family. And Millard will stay with you."

Millard started to protest, then decided not to argue with the king.

"Then it is decided!" said the king with enthusiasm. "You may call for your friends next Saturday, Dusty."

As Dusty and Musty left the gypsy camp Musty said, "I was hoping he'd ask us to stay too. They seem to have such a good time there."

"I just hope everything goes well and this family gets back together. That will be enough for me," answered Dusty.

Musty looked at her brother, who had expressed such concern for their wealthy friends. She too was concerned that the king's experiment work.

THE GYPSIES' SECRET

"Hold onto him, son," yelled Murdoch Mole to Millard.

The boy mole, his pants rolled up to the knees, was reeling in a huge fish from the river.

"Splendid, Millard!" Mrs. Murdoch laughed. "That's the most beautiful fish I've ever seen!"

"It sure is a beaut," the boy mole cried happily.

Murdoch picked up the bucket of bait and the other fish they'd caught and started through the clearing. "We've got enough for the celebration tonight," he said. "Let's get back so they can get them cooking."

Happily the mother and father mole and their son trudged back to the gypsy camp.

"I'm so sorry to be going home," said the mother. "I don't know when I've felt so rested."

"Or had a better time," added the father.

"Me too!" agreed Millard. "But you know, I'm glad to be going home now."

"Are you really, son?" asked his father, slipping his paw easily about the shoulders of the boy.

"Yes, Dad. I really mean it. Now that we've learned to be a family I can't wait. It's been such fun working

and playing together."

"I'm so glad we don't have to put up with those stuffed-shirt servants anymore," said the mother mole. "It was good you fired them all, Murdoch."

"They needed to be let go," agreed her husband. "I think that butler's been stealing from us ever since we hired him. And did I tell you I stopped ordering the flowers from upstairs, dear?" asked Murdoch.

"No, you didn't," she answered in surprise. "Why?"

"Well, this was supposed to have been a surprise when we get home, but I can't keep it. I asked Dusty Mole and his gang to help us out. This week Dusty and his friends have made the rose garden into a baseball diamond. It should be completed by the time we get home."

"Oh, wow! I can't believe it, Dad! Thanks a heap!" said Millard, throwing his fishy paws around his father. That Mystery Club gang has become such good friends to me. I don't think I'll ever be lonely again," cried the happy little mole.

"They are all coming over the day after we get home for a picnic and ball game," said Murdoch happily. "I can't get over how much we've missed as a family by just being so busy. It's not going to happen again."

"We probably won't be able to get your father to go to work at all when we get home," teased the mother.

"Yeah, he'll just want to fish all the time." Millard laughed.

"Not on your life," said Murdoch. "I'll have a lot to do—like the gardening and the butlering and—"

"And the cooking," said the mother happily. "Don't forget, I've never cooked in my life. I've got a lot to learn."

"We'll be patient, won't we, son?" said Murdoch.

"You bet," answered the boy mole, with a happiness he felt he couldn't hold. "We'll help you, Mom. It'll be fun together."

Later, the gypsies and their guests sat around the campfire far into the night. The fire burned low as the violins played and sleepy voices sang softly.

Millard leaned his head on his father's shoulder and felt himself cradled by his dad's arm. Mother Mole sat humming softly, holding her son's paw in her own. Dusty, Musty, Mother Miranda, and Father, who had been invited to the special time celebrating the restored family, were also enjoying the campfire and singing.

Looking across the fire, Murdoch gazed deep into the eyes of the king of the gypsies. Murdoch was so grateful to the kind king for all he had done to bring their family back together. He and his family now knew

the gypsies' secret of love. *Tomorrow, before we leave, I will thank these dear friends for sharing their wonderful secret,* thought Murdoch. *But I will not thank them with money. I will thank them with love.*

THROUGH THE SPYGLASS

Come take a peek through my spyglass, and let's see what's happening to Murdoch Mole and his family now. Since visiting the gypsy camp, the Murdoch Moles are a changed family. The gypsies' secret of love is transforming their unhappy home to one of joy. It almost seems as though they aren't the same animals. Millard Mole is now a member of the Molehole Mystery Club and is having the time of his life with his new pals.

The gypsy king and his people have never returned to Molesbury, but Millard keeps hoping they will come back some day. He has never forgotten his time with them and all the wonderful things he and his family learned from the gypsy king.

Dusty, who at first distrusted the gypsies, is learning that you cannot always believe everything you hear. Sometimes you have to see for yourself through "eyes of love." One of the greatest surprises for Dusty was the ransom note King Gao wrote. Musty likes to call that ransom a "ransom of love."

Through that ransom note, the Murdoch Moles and their Mystery Club friends learned a lot about love that boys and girls need to learn as well.

Did you know that a ransom has been paid for you? That's right. The Word of God tells us in Mark 10:45: "For even the Son of man (Jesus Christ) came not to be ministered unto, but to minister, and to give His life a *ransom* for many."

You see, Jesus paid a *love ransom* for you. If you would like to know more about this ransom, you may write to us at the Molehole Mystery Club, and we'll be glad to tell you all about it.

When you write and become a member of Dusty's Molehole Mystery Club, you will also receive our Molehole Mystery Club Newsletter and ID card. There will be mysteries for you to solve and all kinds of fun things to read and do. Let us hear from you so we can send this fun newsletter to you.

'Bye for now. Be sure to look for the next Molehole Mystery Club book at your Christian bookstore. Happy reading!

UNDERGROUND
"DIG-TIONARY"

SHREW (shrōo): Numerous mouse-like mammals having long pointed snouts, small eyes, and velvety fur.

Have you ever seen a shrew? Probably not, for they are very difficult to find. These bundles of energy are mouse-sized and in the same general family.

Do you know how they are different from mice? Most mice have four toes on each foot, while a shrew has five toes. There are many different kinds of shrews, and they vary greatly in color. Most are grayish-brown with a tail that has two colors.

If you want to find a shrew, you should look in wet areas, such as swamps, or along creeks and rivers. Most varieties of these animals live above ground but travel underground looking for food. They make their nests in stumps, under logs, or under piles of brush.

Like moles, they are thought to be "mysterious," because they are hard to find and identify. They have sometimes been known to eat three times their body weight. Greedy little creatures, shrews have very sharp teeth and are often vicious when cornered by other animals.

God has equipped them with the ability to poison their enemies by their bite. This is why the word shrewish has come to mean evil; we may speak of a "shrewish" person.

However, they are not really dangerous animals. In fact, they are considered a friend to the farmer because they eat harmful insects. By this they fulfill the purpose that God, their Creator, had in mind.

JOIN
MOLEHOLE MYSTERY
CLUB

Would you like to join the Molehole Mystery Club? This will entitle you to receive your very own Molehole Mystery Club ID card and Dusty's free newsletter. The newsletter will be filled with clues and mysteries you can solve and lots of fun things to do.

The newsletter will share things with you from God's Word that will help you live a happy life as a child of God. My spyglass shows me some wonderful words from the Bible that you need to remember always.

These verses are the Molehole Mystery Club Motto, and you will need to memorize them to become a member. The words are found in the Bible [1 Thessalonians 5:21 and 22]: "Test everything. Hold on to the good. Avoid [stay away from] every kind of evil" *(New International Version)*.

We'll be looking for your membership application for our club. See you in the next Molehole adventure story. Happy reading!

MOLEHOLE MYSTERY SERIES

Dusty and Musty are at it again, solving more mysteries. And you can be a part of the fun!

Join in with Dusty and the rest of the club and experience lots of neat adventures with them in **Dusty Mole, Private Eye; Secret at Mossy Root Mansion; The Gypsies' Secret; Foul Play at Moler Park; The Upstairs Connection;** and **The Hare-Brained Habit.**

All of the books in the Molehole Mystery Series are filled with the underground mystery and intrigue of your junior agent friends Dusty and Musty Mole and the rest of the Mystery Club: Morty, Millard, Alby, Penney, Snarkey, Alfred, and Otis.

Don't let the villianous Sammy Shrew catch you by surprise. You can be on the inside track by joining the Molehole Mystery Club.

If you would like to be a member of the Molehole Mystery Club and hear more about the adventures of Dusty and Musty, fill out the card below and send it in. By being an official member, you will receive six issues of the newsletter, *The Underground Gazette,* and your own I.D. card.

MOLEHOLE MYSTERY CLUB MEMBERSHIP APPLICATION

DATE:_____

NAME: _____

ADDRESS: _____

CITY, STATE: _____ ZIP:_____

AGE: _____ BIRTHDATE: _____

___ CHECK HERE IF YOU HAVE MEMORIZED
      OUR MOTTO VERSES,

1 THESSALONIANS 5:21 - 22.
"Test everything. Hold on to the good. Stay
away from every kind of evil."

Wait a minute, you mean the card is missing! Well you can still be a member of the Molehole Mystery Club by just sending in your name and address to:

Molehole Mystery Club
Lock Box 10064
Chicago, IL 60610-0064

Place
Stamp
Here

Molehole Mystery Club
Lock Box 10064
Chicago, IL 60610-0064